*For my mother and father.*
*Without them, Snow Moon is merely a dream.*

# SNOW MOON

## Nicholas Brunelle

Viking

The night sugary snow
fell from the sky,
magical feathers whirled
through my bedroom window.

From outside, in the winter chill,
I saw eyes as dark as chocolate
and feathers cloaked in icy flakes.

From outside, in the winter chill,
I saw eyes as dark as chocolate
and feathers cloaked in icy flakes.

The flurries faded when the ghostly creature lifted its giant wings and soared through the air.

I raced down the stairs
and out the door,
as the wind whispered
snowflakes through the trees.

I followed through forests

And fields of rolled hay,

Over rocks and white hills

All along Crescent Bay,

Beyond the Great Cypress,

Just over Star Bridge,

To a place long forgotten—
a place called Owl Ridge.

There, from all around
the sleeping world,
hundreds of owls
twisted and twirled
across the moonlit sky.

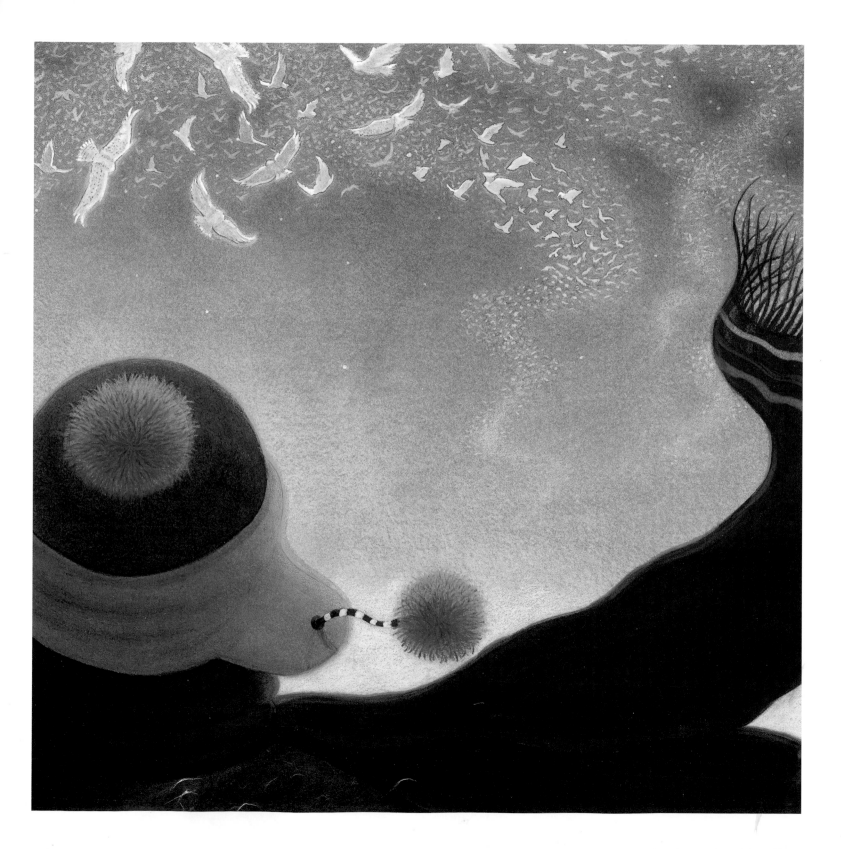

Circling the moon,
they brushed off the light
with a touch of their wings.

And once more that night,
sugary snow fell from the sky.

*Special thanks to Jerry Pinkney*
*for his unique insight and guidance*

VIKING
Published by Penguin Group
Penguin Young Readers Group, 345 Hudson Street, New York, New York 10014, U.S.A.
Penguin Group (Canada), 10 Alcorn Avenue, Toronto, Ontario, Canada M4V 3B2
(a division of Pearson Penguin Canada Inc.)
Penguin Books Ltd, 80 Strand, London WC2R 0RL, England
Penguin Ireland, 25 St Stephen's Green, Dublin 2, Ireland
(a division of Penguin Books Ltd)
Penguin Group (Australia), 250 Camberwell Road, Camberwell, Victoria 3124, Australia
(a division of Pearson Australia Group Pty Ltd)
Penguin Books India Pvt Ltd, 11 Community Centre, Panchsheel Park, New Delhi - 110 017, India
Penguin Group (NZ), Cnr Airborne and Rosedale Roads, Albany, Auckland, New Zealand
(a division of Pearson New Zealand Ltd)
Penguin Books (South Africa) (Pty) Ltd, 24 Sturdee Avenue, Rosebank, Johannesburg 2196, South Africa

Penguin Books Ltd, Registered Offices: 80 Strand,
London WC2R 0RL, England

First published in 2005 by Viking,
a division of Penguin Young Readers Group

1  3  5  7  9  10  8  6  4  2

Copyright © Nicholas Brunelle, 2005

LIBRARY OF CONGRESS CATALOGING-IN-PUBLICATION DATA
Brunelle, Nicholas.
Snow moon / by Nicholas Brunelle.
p. cm.
Summary: One wintry night, a child awakens to find at his window a mysterious owl
that beckons, and together the two set off on a moonlit journey to a place called Owl Ridge.
ISBN 0-670-06024-0 (hardcover)
[1. Owls—Fiction. 2. Bedtime—Fiction. 3. Snow—Fiction.]  I. Title.
PZ7.B8285244Sno 2005
[E]—dc22
2005003926

Manufactured in China  ✳  Set in Colwell Roman